Rosie & the Bear Flag

by Harry Knill

illustrated by Nick Taylor & Donna Neary

stories of **California's flags** from the end
of Spanish rule to the beginning of the United States'

& the story of the
BEAR FLAG REPUBLIC
as seen through the eyes of young
Rosalía Leese, who was there

and an amazing description of how Rosalía Leese and
her mother, *Doña* Rosalía, and *Doña* Francesca,
(sister and wife of General Vallejo)
fool Captain Frémont & the Bear Flag Men
& how everything works out well in the end
(except for a very tragical postscript)

The Bear Flag as described to Pio Pico, Santa Barbara, June 29, 1846. It was similarly described by Larkin: "Mr. Ide and party have a white flag, red fly end, with one star and a Bear in the Union."

Flag of Fremont's California Battalion of Mounted Riflemen raised for the second expedition against the native Californians in arms in Southern California, Winter 1846-47: painted on a blue field.

ARRIEN LA BANDERA !

The Last Day of the glorious Flag of Spain in Alta California

September 29, 1822

Flag: red-yellow-red; red lion on white, yellow castle on red. Uniforms: the canon's: crimson gown & cap, pink mantle, white surplice, gold order, cross, necklace of Guadalupe, green-white-red sash; Governor Sola: dark blue uniform with crimson sash, gold lace on hat, epaulette, cuffs, sword hilt. Imperial soldiers (except the buglers): dark blue coatees with red collars, cuffs, turnbacks; white breeches; red pom-pons; black shakos (hats), cartridge boxes, shoes, sword scabbards; yellow brass chin scales, buttons, sword hilts & scabbard tips. Bugler (Imperial cavalryman with the visiting dignitaries): red coatee, blue collar, cuffs, turnbacks; blue trousers with red stripe; white belt.

Canon Fernandez & Governor Sola

Flag of the Mexican Empire

The Spanish Viceroy sent General Iturbide to put down the revolt in Mexico against Spain. But instead of stopping the revolution, Iturbide joined it—and in May 1822 he proclaimed himself Emperor of the Empire of Mexico. Alta California was far away from the Capital, and it was not until September that an Imperial Commissioner, the Reverend Canon Don Augustin Fernandez de San Vicente, wearing the costume of the new Order of Guadalupe, arrived at Monterey with a large number of military officers, to announce the change of flags. The *canonigo* was received magnificently by Governor Sola, who knew that not an inch of soil of New Spain remained in Spanish hands. Governor Sola examined carefully the canon's credentials, and found them all in order. The canon then made a mighty speech about the benefits of the famous Plan of Iguala with its Three Guarantees of religion, independence, and union. He made all the soldiers swear to support the new order and then, with an honor guard of the cavalry company, marching very slowly, he went to the flag pole upon which waved the glorious Standard of Castile.

Around the flagpole a square was formed: to the east were the artillerymen, to the south the infantry, to the north dismounted cavalry, and to the west, civil officials and all the people. At 11:00, amidst a deadly silence, the canon's voice of thunder shouted," Strike the colors" (*"Arrien la bandera!"*). Immediately that standard which for fifty-three years had proudly waved over Alta California was lowered. Many old soldiers wept. The national colors of the Three Guarantees were run up, and when the new flag unfurled, Canon Fernandez shouted, *"Viva la independencia Mejicana!* Hurrah for the three guarantees!" There were some cheers, and then Lieutenant Estudillo (you remember him from *Dos Californios*) ordered a 21-gun salute and three salvos of musketry. And, when the Esselen Indians saw an eagle painted on the new flag, they were greatly delighted, for the eagle was their sacred bird.

Afterwards everyone went off to the beautiful church of San Carlos. Then there was a fiesta with foot races for the tall, strong Esselin Indians, horse races for the rancheros, and in the evening Governor

Flag: green-white-red, brown & white eagle, gold crown, green cactus

Luis Antonio Argüello, Governor from 1822 to 1825

Gov. Echeandía: green coat with bright red breast; gilt epaulettes, embroidery & buttons; flag: white field & blue oval & scroll (the colors of Montezuma); gold scroll & leaf work; brown trees, green leaves, blue sky, green ocean, etc.

1827

MOCTEZUMA

José Maria Echeandía, Governor Nov. 1825 to Jan. 1831, and again Dec. 1831 to Jan. 1833

Sola held a ball. There the *canonigo*, in a booming voice heard far away, won the people over by telling them that Iturbide was none other than the representative of King Ferdinand of Spain, who would in a short time come to Mexico and take over the reins of his empire and look after the California missions.

Soon Emperor Iturbide was no more; a republic took his place in 1823. The crown came off the Mexican eagle, who found instead a snake to chew, and branches of laurel and oak to hold. Canon Fernandez later found his way to Santa Fe, New Mexico, where he became vicar.

The Californians soon felt neglected by the new government in Mexico. So Joaquin de la Torre proposed lowering the Mexican flag and running up in its place an independent flag. This would have a white field with a blue oval in the center, with an Indian inside wearing a feathered headdress and carrying a bow and a quiver of arrows, stepping across the Bering Strait—the way America was thought to have been peopled. The oval would be supported by an olive tree, the symbol of peace, and an oak tree, symbol of strength. The name of Alta California would be changed to MOCTEZUMA—a proposal made July 7, 1827 by Governor Echeandia himself! The Territorial Deputation approved, and a notice was sent to Mexico. And that was the end of that.

In 1830 Manuel Victoria was appointed governor. He tried to stop the grabbing up of the rich mission lands. The Californians didn't like this, or his tyrannical ways—such as shooting people, and not calling the assembly. The Californians, led by Pio Pico and Juan Bandini of San Diego, rebelled. At a battle on December 5, 1831, near Cahuenga, between San Fernando and Los Angeles, Victoria was badly wounded by the rebel lancers. He was treated by an American at San Gabriel; here he surrendered, and asked to go back to Mexico. There he reported that "there was great danger of an attempt to separate the territory of Alta California from Mexico."

Soon Governor Figueroa was sent up from Mexico to rule California, and the Californians loved him. "His characteristics were generosity, philanthropy, love for his fellow man, and a sense of justice that could never be surpassed," wrote Alvarado. But, alas, the good governor died in 1833, and his successors were not liked at all. Governor Chico came in 1836 and brought with him the new Mexican Centralist Constitution of General Santa Anna, replacing the Federal Constitution of 1824, which Alvarado called the Magna Carta of all their liberties. Governor Chico, nicknamed "the Bear," and said to be as "insolent as Nero," was totally dominated by his lady friend, *Doña* Cruz. After three months of bothersome rule, he was chased away, and succeeded by Gutierrez. This ruler became immediately known as "Chico's heir," and was also a Centralist—of the Mexican party then unpopular in California.

Juan B. Alvarado, a young customs clerk, inspired by his boss, the rascally Customs Director, Angel Ramirez, led a revolution in Monterey against the new Central system, or rather, for freedom for California from Mexico. He had on his side José Castro, Captain Hinckley (a Yankee with a band of musicians on board his ship) and the famous backwoodsman, Isaac Graham, who joined most of the California revolutions in those days. Captain Graham ran a whisky still near San Juan Bautista, and his fierce reputation was worth many men. He led a troop of dead-aim American *rifeleros*.

The little army pretended that Lieutenant Vallejo, who commanded the Sonoma outpost, was coming, too (he arrived, but later). They captured the hill fort above Monterey, and aimed a gun with the only cannon ball they had at Governor Gutierrez in the Presidio below. After studying a book about cannonading, with the help of some brandy, Cosme Peña aimed the ball: it landed at the very toes of Governor Gutierrez. The governor surrendered, and was put on a ship for the desert tip of Baja California.

Figueroa had warned, too, about a clique plotting to separate California from Mexico. Now it had come to pass. "You...boldly waved the banner of the free: FEDERATION OR DEATH," pronounced the new Governor on November 6, 1836 to the new citizens of the FREE AND SOVEREIGN STATE OF CALIFORNIA. "Let us be united, Californios, and we shall be invincible."..."California is Free," shouted everyone. But united?

The only seal of the *Free State*; March 9, 1837

Alvarado's Banner of the Glorious Revolution
of November 6, 1836
Red letters on a white field, is a fair guess.

Alvarado had great power of speech and argument.
Later, in 1845, Alvarado was described by Dr. Wood as having long, black whiskers.

The Lone Star Flag

This is "a Country whose inhabitants are desirous of becoming an independent nation. The Governor General has been expelled from the territory...and a new *Star* appeared."
—*A. Robinson*, December 18, 1836

"We see the gleam of the *Star* which will guide us to our prosperity." —*Alvarado*

"Affairs in California are still rather revolting."

Alfred Robinson, May 5, 1836

It was said that a LONE STAR FLAG had been made in California, and that Alvarado had actually talked about raising it over the Monterey Presidio. We all know what the Lone Star Flag meant in Texas. Such a flag is preserved in the Southwest Museum, in Los Angeles.

Governor Gutierrez had wanted Juan Bandini of San Diego to be the Customs Director—the only person in all California who could put his hands on real money (everyone else used hides and tallow as currency). This is why the existing Customs Director Angel Ramirez, a famous schemer, concocted the Monterey revolution led by Alvarado. The citizens of San Diego wanted the Customs House moved there, and the money with it. They were all against Alvarado's new Independent government, which would surely keep the old Customs House right where it had always been, in Monterey. So the *Dieguenos* decided it was their turn to revolt, and they revolted against Alvarado. Pio Pico even accused Alvarado of leading his revolution for the United States. Pico was from San Diego, and he was trying to make Alvarado unpopular. But Alvarado was not interested in 1837 in "turning California over to the Americans, who were ruled then by the Slavery Party." Instead, he tried to put California under British protection, for he thought that California was about to be sold by Mexico to Russia.

Captain Portilla came up from Baja California and formed a small army of *Dieguenos* and *Angelenos*. But Alvarado and the *Montereyeños* had Santa Barbara on their side. The *Barbareños* cheered Alvarado when he and his little band of soldiers arrived at their beautiful town. Amidst the cheers, the governor thought of unfurling a truly Californian flag at Santa Barbara. "With such a plan in mind I had a Mexican flag brought to my room and on the white part of that banner in letters printed with a brush I wrote the words: Independence for California. When the new banner I proposed to have unfurled had been made ready, I had Lieutenant Peña and Second Lieutenant Dias called...'One of you is to carry this banner to the Santa Barbara Mission. There you will deliver it to Father Duran for him to bless in the church, while the other one is to carry a sky-rocket, and, as soon as the flag has been blessed, he will set off the rocket, so that I may know that we now have a flag of our own. As soon as I see the rocket, I will get out all the troops and all the people and we shall set out to meet you, who, without the loss of a moment's time, will start for the town at full gallop the instant Father Duran has blessed the new flag." The interview with Father Duran did not last long, for he explained that he was afraid to compromise the Franciscan friars throughout the entire Mexican Republic. When Governor Alvarado heard this, he became downcast and thought for a moment of making an ally of some sea pirate, many of whom were still roaming about at that time. The flag became well used, anyway.

January 3, 1837

See back cover for colors.

INDEPENDENCIA DE CALIFORNIA

Lieutenants Peña & Diaz

Father Duran

Alvarado knew the temperament of the Southerners. He thought it best to take a large band of musicians on his campaign against Los Angeles (the *Angelenos* were causing trouble because they wanted the capital moved to their town) and San Diego, where the music would bring merriment and rejoicing. After a single cannon shot at San Fernando, the enemy ran away. Alvarado marched freely into Los Angeles and brought to an end, for a little while, the misunderstanding which existed between the inhabitants of the northern and southern districts.

But in a short time, some bad citizens stirred up discord again and civil war broke out anew. The sly Angel Ramirez seized the Monterey Presidio—now he was mad at Alvarado for not jailing Bandini. And Carlos Carrillo had a brother, José Antonio, whom Governor Figueroa had sent to the Congress in Mexico City, just to get him out of California. José Antonio told President Bustamonte that if his brother Carlos was appointed governor, the revolt in California would end without the cost of an army being sent there. Late in 1837 Carlos heard of his appointment at his "capital" of Los Angeles, whereupon he declared San Diego the new home of the Customs House.

San Buenaventura; three cheers to that town for finally restoring its proper name!!!

Alvarado didn't like this—and he still had Santa Barbara on his side, even though that was the Carrillos' town. Alvarado refused to turn over the government—the president had forgotten to sign Carrillo's appointment, he said. Alvarado sent a clever agent, Captain Castillero, to Mexico City to see if Mexico would approve of him as the true Governor of Alta California. With revolts to the north, and with revolts to the south, and momentarily expecting a Mexican army coming up after him, Alvarado had decided it was perhaps best to go back to Mexico, after all. On July 9, 1837, Alvarado and the Santa Barbara citizens took an oath to the Central Government— the very one they had revolted from. But Alta California had been raised to a Department of Mexico, and was no longer a lowly Territory. This meant that it could now send a voting member to the National Congress.

Captain Castillero brought back an order from Mexico: Alvarado was indeed to be governor. Carrillo didn't like this, and decided to march with an army and take Santa Barbara. There, the *Barbareños* drove the *Carrillistas* back to San Buenaventura, where they fortified themselves. José Castro took down the cannon from Santa Barbara and fired at the church, which was assaulted at dawn. Inside, hiding, was found none other than Jose Antonio Carrillo.

The Santa Barbara Flag was at the Battle of San Buenaventura, where it "perched" over the victory won by the Northerners with the use of their CULEBRINA. This was a huge monster gun made of bronze, which battered down the church doors with cannon balls weighing 36 pounds.

The monster CULEBRINA, and new uniforms just received.

¡SI·LOS·ENEMIGOS·NO·SE·RINDEN·LOS·HARE·DEGOLLAR!!

Flag of San Juan Capistrano
at Las Flores, April 21, 1838

Red hat bands & scroll on flag (no
quarter would be given!); white field &
letters on flag; black hats, blue jackets
& pants (*calzoneras*), silver epaulettes &
buttons, red sash & collars.

Manuel Cantua

Capt. Salvador Vallejo

Carlos Carrillo himself escaped. Lieutenant Colonel Tovar, who had now come up from Baja California, met Carrillo at San Diego and from there they both went north with their troops to San Juan Capistrano. From there they were chased back to Las Flores, an old mission branch not far south (today only ruins of it are found at Camp Pendleton). They were met there by troops of the Northern army, led by the grand Salvador Vallejo, of colossal strength and stature. Upon reaching Las Flores, Captain Vallejo had taken from his saddle bags a monstrous flag of white linen, with a red scroll. When it unfurled to the breeze, the following words were seen to be inscribed in the center: IF OUR ENEMIES DO NOT SURRENDER, I SHALL HAVE THEM BEHEADED. This standard was placed in the hands of a soldier named Manuel Cantua (who later declared himself governor, when Pio Pico and Castro fled in 1846). When the enemy saw this monstrous flag, Tovar and his troops fled to Mexico, and Carlos Carrillo surrendered. Carlos Carrillo, like Sancho Panza, was given an island to govern; his was Santa Rosa, instead of all Alta California.

Sometimes people didn't bother to paint their message on a flag before sending it up the pole. At Monterey, in 1839, Governor Alvarado woke up on a fine February morning to find an enormous skull hanging from the flag halyard. This curse of daring enemies succeeded in terrifying the Governor's household. His French chef, Raoul, refused to serve lunch or any other meal, and hastily took the next ship south.

A Los Angeles (or *Los Diablos*) Flag Story

Don Abel Sterns, a Yankee from Massachusetts, was the first merchant to export hides from Alta California. He lived at Los Angeles. The Prefect there was *Don* Cosme Peña, a friend of Alvarado's. That governor had not been popular in the south, as you know, and among the *Angelenos* were many rowdy souls—so many that *Don* Cosme re-christened the city 'Los Diablos.' A number of these young devils found fault with the prefect for having his office at the American Stern's house. On a Sunday morning they met and pulled down the departmental flag, then tied a bull to the pole, all with noise and confusion. Peña, away at San Pedro, returned and had some of the culprits put in the calaboose while others went and hid, and soldiers were brought from Santa Barbara to quiet the fuss. The citizens complained, Peña quit, the governor up in Monterey was annoyed, the boys were each fined five pesos, the councilmen each ten pesos. The rascally *Angelenos* really thought the capital belonged in their tipsy town (no old-time source says anything good about them.)

14

The Last Days of the
Flag of the Russian American Company
in Alta California
July, 1840

"The result of it all is that the Russians are going to evacuate this year the establishments of Ross and Bodega."—*M. Vallejo* Declining business had something to do with it, too.

Left: white, blue, red stripes; brown eagle with yellow beaks & claws, gold & silver crowns, scepter, orb & chain; below, blue cross of St. Andrew on a white field.

Manager Rotchef, *Alférez* Piña and his men at Fort Ross

In 1840 Bodega was nearly deserted by the Russians, so General Vallejo sent Alferez Piña there to prevent smuggling. But an American captain said that Manager Rotchef at Fort Ross claimed Bodega as a free Russian port. Piña was then sent to tell Rotchef that Bodega belonged to Mexico and not to Russia, even though Russian ships had been tolerated. Rotchef, furious when he found Mexican soldiers there, raised the Russian flag and dared the Californians to pull it down; he told them to leave or be shot.

The Stars & Stripes on the Sacramento River

Captain Phelps, of the Boston ship *Alert*, sailed his cutter up the Sacramento River in July 1840 and claimed that this was "the first time the Stars and Stripes waved over its waters." But actually Captain Davis had sailed up the river in 1839 with the schooners *Isabel* and *Nicholas*, taking that soon-to-be famous Swiss gentleman, Captain Sutter, to the junction of the American and Sacramento Rivers; those vessels were flying American colors. When Captain Phelps did arrive at the new establishment, he was welcomed there with a gorgeous display of all the flags that Sutter could gather from his neighbors and ships visiting California.

Sutter soon began to think about becoming free of Mexico, too. He wrote to Jacob Leese the following year: "The people don't know me yet, but soon they will find out what I am able to do...The first step they do against me is that I will make declaration of Independence and proclaim California a Republique independent of Mexico."

Sutter's gorgeous display of flags at his new establishment

July 30, 1840

I sympathized with and respected the Americans who came to this new empire. It was of such men that I planned to build New Helvetia into a sovereign state.
—John A. Sutter

NOEVA HELVECIA

CAPT. SUTTER

Flags: Mexico's Naval flag (no eagle), Old Glory, Russian American Co's—the colors of these are all familiar to you; next: Chile's (most ships on the coast went there then), white & red stripes (Texas' flag was similar, but he wouldn't have dared raise that), France's: blue, white, red; & Switzerland's: white cross in a red field.

A trapper and one of Sutter's Hawaiian lady friends   Captains Phelps & Sutter & Sutter's bulldog

Jacob Leese & Rosalía Vallejo

Jacob Leese was born in Ohio about 1809. When he was twenty, he went down the Mississippi River and up the Arkansas, and joined Captain Rogers' Company of Trappers. He had many dangerous adventures in the wild mountains, where the Indians were sometimes unfriendly. Resting from these, he took a job at Bent & St. Vrain's Trading Post at Taos, New Mexico. Here he heard stories about the wealth of California, and especially about its excellent mules—which were worth fortunes in the eastern United States. So soon off west he went with a band of New Mexicans, famous in those days as most expert horse and mule thieves. In 1833, by way of the Rio Grande and the Colorado Rivers, he arrived at San Gabriel Mission, in Alta California. He came with an introduction to the good Governor Figueroa.

Governor Figueroa had just been at San Gabriel, where he met William Richardson; the two talked about establishing a new pueblo on the San Francisco Bay. Together they sailed north to Monterey, and on board the ship was—Jacob Leese. Richardson went on to the San Francisco Presidio, and from there he soon moved over to Yerba Buena Cove, where he built a little shack to be his headquarters as Port Captain. Leese visited him there, and thought it a fine place for a store for supplying the ranchos. By the by, *Alcalde* de Haro came over from the Presidio, and together with Richardson, they laid out the new pueblo. The first street would be called *Calle de la Fundacion*.

Leese made a partnership with Nathan Spear and Captain Hinckley to open a store at Yerba Buena, and with a grant of land from Governor Chico, they put up a building on the *Calle de la Fundacion*, next door to Richardson's tent-building. The store was built of redwood and may have been pre-fabricated, because it took little time to complete. A grand fiesta was held to celebrate the new enterprise on the Fourth of July, and guests came from all the ranchos around the Bay. Captain Steel, an early trader on the coast, and Captain Vioget were there; the Estudillos, the Martinez, Captain Richardson, the Castros, the Guerreros, the de Haros, too. General Vallejo came from Sonoma and brought his tall, witty, charming, rich, beautiful sister, *Doña* Rosalía. Two small guns were brought over from the Presidio for the fireworks, and Captain Hinckley had with him his famous band of musicians from Hawaii. The party, with grand dinners, dances, and toasts galore, lasted for two days.

The 4th of July in old Yerba Buena, 1836

"Jacob P. Leese was the first settler who came after me. He built his house on July 3, 1836." —*Capt. Richardson* "I have concluded to stop in this place for Good in con-sequence of the great Prospect ahead which is plainly seen...the Present house is open and So much Exposed that I am afraid to leave it alone." —*J. Leese*, Aug. 3, 1836

Don Wardaloopy, as Jacob Leese called General M. Guadalupe Vallejo, had wanted his sister to marry *Don* Timothy Murphy, who administered the lands of San Rafael Mission. But *Don Timotheo*, who had a pack of hounds sent over from Ireland, was preoccupied hunting the great elk nearby. One day when General Vallejo was away from Sonoma, *Doña* Rosalía, travelling by back roads from Monterey, arrived at Sonoma and was married right then and there at the Mission by Padre Quijas, who was not fond of the general. She married her host of the Fourth of July—*Don Luis* Leese. When the townspeople discovered the marriage, the *fiesta* began, and it lasted until the general arrived. The general was furious! He did not like to miss weddings. He called Rosalía his favorite sister, because he admired her independence. *Don Luis* took Mrs. Leese to Yerba Buena, having done this "something of the sly," as he called his method of marrying. His store bartered hides and tallow, and also beef, wheat, flour, skins—the products of California—for chairs, fiddle strings, flat irons, nails, hinges, knives, ovens, kettles, hammers, pots, chests of drawers, champagne, toilet water, tea, sugar, coffee, spices, buckets, hats, needles, blankets, buttons, handker-chiefs, sheets, calico, shirts, shoes, trousers, stockings, etc.,

Don Luis built a launch, the *Isabella*, at Napa, for trading on the Carquinez Straits and the Sacramento River. And, on the 19th of April, 1838, a fine daughter was born, christened Rosalía Domitela de Jesus Leese. A larger house was now needed,

and one was built on what is now the west side of Montgomery Street, between Clay and Sacramento Streets, in San Francisco.

The partnership of SPEAR, LEESE & HINCKLEY ended in 1839. Leese's accounting did not appeal to his partners, nor did his wheat dealings with the Russians. Captain Hinckley wasn't always nice to do business with, anyway. Now *Don Luis* went into business with Captain Salvador Vallejo, whom you've already read about. Together they built another launch, the *Rosalía*, to trade with the Russians, and a warehouse next to the foot of what is now Broadway. The Russian warehouse burned down, and then the Tsar decided to abandon California altogether.

Once Leese helped drive a huge herd of cattle from Sonoma to Fort Vancouver. The drovers assembled at Cache Creek, where they met under an American flag tied up on a cottonwood tree. Our flag was already to be found deep inside California in 1842. In fact, the earliest raising of the U.S. flag in California is supposed to have been in 1828, when Captain A.B. Thompson of the schooner *Washington* from Maine raised it in San Diego to celebrate his arrival.

The Hudson's Bay Company
& Rae's End

Jacob Leese's business prospered at Yerba Buena Cove. Then the rich Hudson's Bay Company offered him a choice of competition or a sale to them. He sold, for $4,600. The Leeses had a lovely rancho, Huichica, at Sonoma, and Jacob opened a store on the Plaza which still remains. It is now called Fitch House, at 487 Front Street. He also bought the Novato Rancho north of San Rafael. The agent for the H.B. Company said that they had spent 75,000 pounds to drive the New England firm of Bryant & Sturgis from the California Coast, and they would spend a million to drive out all other Yankees, if necessary.

The British now had a choice headquarters at the best post on the coast. But the most unfavorable weather in memory—no rain at all and a total failure of crops, plus 14 busy Yankee ships competing in spite of threats, dampened the prospects of the H.B. Company. And worse, General Vallejo became very difficult to deal with, as he apparently favored the Americans. Soon Sir George Simpson of the H.B. Company decided to shut down the post at "that wretched place of Yerba Buena" because of "the unwillingness of the people of California to do any business that is likely to prove advantageous to the Company...the sooner we break off all communication with California the better," he wrote. It will, "to a moral certainty, sooner or later, fall into the possession of Americans."

The H.B. Company post had been quite successful up to January 1845, when Rae, the agent, fell in love with a California lady and, when caught, shot himself. He left a note: "The Company ought to blame themselves, for they have entirely neglected the California trade." Rae had also helped Alvarado in the battles with Micheltórena, and thought he had put the Company in hot water. The store was sold to Mellus & Howard in 1845, and it soon made those young men very rich.

It was "a wood house, built of the old Dutch form."
—*Capt. Henry Pierce*

Agent Rae

Flag: British Union of red crosses of Saints George & Patrick, white cross of Saint Andrew against blue; red field with white letters

22

Jones' Mistake
October 20 & 21, 1842

In the thinking of the day, it was America's "manifest destiny" to get a hold of the continent's western side. Americans living in California were increasing in numbers, and together with visiting sailors they stirred up plenty of interest in California back home. But there were also British and French eyes looking hopefully at California, and their owners were not impressed with President Monroe's 1823 doctrine, which said, "No European Government should plant colonies in North America," (as Thomas Larkin explained it). In 1835, when Andrew Jackson was president, an offer was made by the U.S. Government to buy California for $5,000,000. This would have been accepted, it was said, if the British diplomats hadn't foiled the deal. But it was becoming clear to everyone that California wouldn't remain with Mexico for long, for the civil wars there caused a lack of interest in such a far away place.

Some Californians favored Britain, some favored France, but the U.S.' friends were the largest group, probably. They heard that Britain had lent Mexico $7,000,000 and that California was to be the security for the loan. Britain could easily get California in this way, or by being first on the spot if war started. Texas was going to become part of the United States and Mexico was certain to become furious; and war could break out. Then California would be fair game for all. A British squadron was in the Pacific with four great ships; a French squadron was there with eight ships. Commodore Thomas Ap Catesby Jones commanded the Pacific squadron of the United States, with only five ships, much smaller than the British. "These Britishers shall never get possession of California," said Commodore Wilkes of the U.S. Exploration Squadron when he was here in 1841 with six ships and 600 men, "we are their equal and a little more."

Commodore Jones, at Peru, heard from the U.S. consul up at Mazatlán that war was about to break out, and he read in a Boston newspaper quoting one from New Orleans that Mexico was selling California to Britain. He decided that the U.S. and Mexico were at war, that the English admiral was on his way to take California, and that it was Jones' duty to get there first. The frigate *United States* and the Sloop of War *Cyane* made all sail possible for California. On October 18, 1842, they anchored off Monterey. They sailed into the harbor flying British colors, to fool the Californians in case they had already become British. They saw that the British squadron had not yet arrived.

The Californians on shore had not heard of a war. But the captain of the American ship *Fame* had heard rumors of one in Hawaii, and that Britain was buying California. "A concatenation of unforeseen and unforeseeable events required prompt and energetic action," said Jones, and he sent Captain Armstrong ashore to demand a surrender to the United States. Alvarado read the demand, "and after a long silence while he first turned pale and then red as if his blood was about to break through his eyes, with a trembling voice full of impatience he told Armstrong that he was a Spaniard and even if he had half the strength of the Commodore, he would consider

The fort dubbed Fort Catesby —bah!

The Chieftain of Monterey is a humbugging old fudge.
—Gunner Meyers of the *Cyane*. Indeed, if Alvarado bothered to look for the newspapers, instead of hiding behind the pool table, he could have spared this embarassing scene. His predecessor, Gutierrez, had handled Commodore Kennedy, USN, far better when he came in 1836, looking for an excuse to take Monterey.

But I may be wrong.

Captain
Armstrong

All uniforms are navy blue; black shakos on marines, gold epaulettes on officers, white belts

it equal," wrote Osio, who was there. Alvarado then asked about the defences and was told that they "were of no consequence, as everyone knows." Surrender was decided upon. A few minutes after the scene here, the Stars and Stripes were flying on the flagpole.

But, whoa! The next day, Jones borrowed some recent papers from Mexico and read that the two countries were still friendly, and that a sale to England was not so. Jones lowered the American flag and rehoisted Mexico's with proper ceremony. "I regret in the surrender the loss to the United States of the beautiful women of California," said he. But Jones considered that his capture gave the United States the first right in the future.

"The whole of this Affair appeared at the same time a dream. No one could realize it; no one understood why the Country was taken or why returned to its former owners; there is none here or but few believe that the reading of those Mexican papers had any effect on the Commodore's mind. They believe that the taking & surrendering of this country was both planned out at one time: for what purpose they cannot fathom. They suspect that in time there may be a dispute about this Country between England & France and the States and the fact that the States having had their flag flying here 24 hours may avail them something hereafter. The Commodore says he came without orders from Washington. This is not much believed by these people." T.O. Larkin

"For many years before California was annexed, the impression seemed to exist in the United States Pacific squadron, that its most important purpose was to occupy California...The British squadron seemed to have an equally strong idea that its business was to prevent any such act upon the part of ours...In the fall of 1844, we lay in the harbor of Monterey, ready to take California, upon the first intelligence justifying it; in 1845, we did the same thing, and in 1846 it was taken...this event was decreed long before the administration under which it was accomplished...."

Dr. Wm. Wood, Surgeon of the
Pacific Squadron

General Micheltorena
& the Battle of Cahuenga,
February 21, 1845

"In 1842 the Mexican Government was convinced that the United States needed the territory of Alta California and would get it either by peaceful means or by force. An army under General Micheltorena was sent, made up of thieves and murderers from several prisons. It was expected that the general could make them into soldiers."—*Osio*. Micheltorena also came up because the Californians were all relatives, and couldn't stop quarrelling long enough to rule themselves. General Vallejo wrote the president to send someone else to do the job.

Micheltorena got off to a bad start. Jones took Monterey while Micheltorena was in Los Angeles. Jones, admitting the mistake, went south to apologize to the general. Micheltorena demanded a full set of musical instruments to equip a band, to forget the matter. Had he been able to get this, he would have had a much easier time ruling the Californians. This wasn't such a silly demand as the Yankees thought. There had

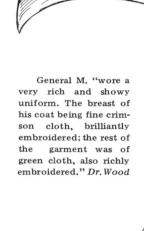

General M. "wore a very rich and showy uniform. The breast of his coat being fine crimson cloth, brilliantly embroidered; the rest of the garment was of green cloth, also richly embroidered." *Dr. Wood*

been no robberies at all when California was independent, Salvador Vallejo said, but when Micheltorena's band arrived, everything that could be carried off, was. Poor California! General Micheltorena was lazy and seldom got up before noon. When his very bad soldiers had eaten all the pigs and chickens in Los Angeles, they came north with the general and soon presented horrible scandals to the good people of Monterey—they even stole the clothes off clotheslines. Pio Pico visited Micheltorena in Monterey, and the general made certain comments which sounded as though he, along with Captain Sutter, intended to declare the independence of Alta California!

But soon, as always, a rebellion against the ruler from Mexico took place. It began at the Salinas River, and the soldiers' conduct was the excuse. A treaty was made at Santa Teresa near San Jose, where General Micheltorena agreed to return the robber soldiers to Mexico. But he did not live up to this. The revolutionists, led by Alvarado, as you'd guess, went south to make friends with their former enemies, the *Angelenos*. There they chose Pio Pico as the new governor. Then they marched to battle against General Micheltorena near a big oak tree at Cahuenga. Alvarado fired the first shot at the enemy "to wake them up," whereupon the general raised a white flag over his shay. He had come to an understanding with José Castro that he'd leave California—he was bored with the difficult Californians anyway—and he wanted to be away before it all fell to the Americans.

The Fleets Competing
on the Pacific Station, after William Meyers of the *Cyane*, 1842

Carysfort (Great Britain)　　　　　*Boussolé* (France)　　　　　*Cyane* (United States)

Years went by in Sonoma and Rosie grew up. José Castro as Commandant General collected all the money from the Customs House at Monterey. Now poor Governor Pico wanted some, but Castro wouldn't spare it. So soon they prepared to do battle with each other. One day early in June 1846, General Castro came to Sonoma to see about horses for invading the south (Sonoma had the reputation of raising the best and largest horses in California). In California at that time, the women could do anything that the men could, and often a good deal more. Rosie went out to help round up the horses.

The Californians often discussed the future of their country and the coming changing of flags. Because of the revolutionary troubles in Mexico, they would have to decide soon whether to become Independent again or have France or Great Britain or the United States protect them. General Vallejo favored the United States, but Castro wanted France (though he told Leese on this visit that he was in favor of the U.S. taking possession!) and Pio Pico wanted Great Britain. It was said that Pio Pico would become a Duke if the British flag should fly here. Pablo de la Guerra wanted to be Independent. "Beware of the Americans," said Castro, "they are capable of changing the color of the very stars." But, said Vallejo, "why should we shrink from incorporating ourselves with the happiest and freest nation in the world...California will grow strong and flourish, and her people will be prosperous, happy and free. Look not with jealousy upon the hardy pioneers who scale our mountains and cultivate our unoccupied plains; but rather welcome them as brothers, who come to share with us a common destiny." Pio Pico had a good point, though: "Shall we consent that the northern republic bring to our soil of liberty the horrible slavery permitted in its States? Shall we suffer human blood sold at a price for vile gain? "

"There is no doubt that France is intriguing to become mistress of California," General Vallejo wrote Alvarado. Sutter was considered a Frenchman, for he had been in the French army, and he often threatened to hoist the French flag and take over the country. Consul Gasquet was sent to represent France in Monterey; this seemed

"Beware of the Americans; they are capable
of changing the color of the very stars." —*Castro*

General Castro visits Sonoma

"Sr. Castro, I believe to have gone North to raise a party against Pico." —*Larkin*, June 1, 1846

very dangerous to the Americans. French war ships visited Monterey and were very well received; Captain La Place of the *Artemise* warned about the U.S. intention to take California. Count Duflot de Mofras went everywhere in California, taking notes, but he didn't help the French cause much. He annoyed nearly everyone, so Salvador Vallejo pulled a prank on him and sent him looking for Mission Santa Rosa. Limantour, another Frenchman, managed to obtain nearly all of Yerba Buena by helping Micheltorena during Alvarado's revolt. But the most important force for French California was José Castro. He didn't like the Americans; "they are so clever that some day they will build ladders that will reach the sky."

In 1846 Monsieur Gasquet called the French squadron to Monterey to obtain satisfaction for (imaginary) insults to one Professor Henri Cambuston. A ship arrived with orders to get tough, but happily the Stars and Stripes were flying when it arrived and the American fleet was anchored in the harbor. "If this had not been the case," said Alvarado, "I think it very probable that the French flag would have been raised on that occasion, as that nation had many sympathizers in the capital of Alta California and in the city of Los Angeles."

"If the French warship had arrived in June rather than in July, its commander would have had not great difficulties to overcome in inducing the inhabitants of the *Departmento* to declare themselves in favor of annexation to France, since by the end of June all Californians were very much alarmed over the outrages the 'Bears' were committing in the northern part."

Fremont arrives in California

James C. Fremont, on his third exploration expedition westward, arrived at Captain Sutter's on the 4th of December, 1845. On the 28th of January, Fremont, with Vice Consul Leidesdorff from Yerba Buena, arrived at the house and store of Consul Larkin in Monterey. The house was indicated by the U.S. Flag flying over it, and by a tin and glass lantern painted red over the door, with *U.S. Consulate* painted in yellow letters on the glass. The next day Larkin wrote Prefect Manuel Castro, "Captain J.C. Fremont of the United States Army...has been ordered to survey the most practicable route from the United States to the Pacific Ocean...he has left his Company of fifty hired men (not of the United States Army) on the frontiers of this Department for the purpose of resting themselves and animals." They then went to see General José Castro, and Larkin explained that Fremont had "come himself to Monterey to obtain clothing and funds to purchase animals and provisions." "Permission was given to him" to do this, said Castro, and to rest his men in the valley of the San Joaquin, and then go on to Oregon. Larkin had worked hard to make the Californians like the United States, and he had good hopes that California would peacefully join our country.

*I am now going on business
to see some gentlemen on the coast
. . . Fremont, January 24, 1846*

Flag: blue eagle, red pipe, white stars & canton;
red & white stripes

*Nothing was
impossible for
Fremont to perform . . .*

Capt. **John C. Fremont**
of the Topographical Engineers,
U S Army, on his 3rd exploration trip
westward, with his famous scout, **Kit Carson,**
& the flag of his 1st exploration expedition of 1842

A famous
call in Monterey
January 29, 1846

General José Castro, a visitor from Sonoma, Consul Larkin, Captain Fremont; Vice-Consul Leidesdorff and Prefect Castro were here, too.

On top of the Gavilan Mountains near San Juan Bautista

"at the head water of a stream which strikes the road to Monterey," March 9th, 1846

In all probability they will attack you . . . it may cause an interruption to business. Larkin March 8

"I am making myself as strong as possible...if we are hemmed in and assaulted here, we will die, every man of us, under the flag of our country." —*J.C. Fremont, March 9, 1846*

"I cannot help but admire the young Captain," wrote Alvarado, "who had the audacity in a wilderness to fling down the gauntlet...I believe now and always have believed that Fremont had orders from his government to proceed as he did."

Kit Carson and Capt. Fremont

Fremont's Folly

"We retired slowly and growlingly." —J. C. Fremont

But Fremont and his 60 men camped in the Santa Clara Valley, where they were rather rude to the citizens, and they made "scandalous skirmishes." He was then ordered out of the Department by Castro. Fremont refused to obey and moved camp to the top of the Gavilan (or Hawk) Mountains, near San Juan Bautista, then called San Juan de Castro, because it was General Castro's home town. There he built a fort and raised the U.S. flag.

Fremont and his men stayed there from the 7th to the 10th of March, then left in the middle of a dark night. The Californians were relieved, for Castro was rounding them up to do battle with these expert American riflemen. The results of an attack would have been deadly. "Castro was not addicted to expose his interesting person to bullets," wrote Señora Casarín.

Next Fremont went to New Helvetia, where earlier he had tried without luck to buy mules from Sutter, the need for which took him to Monterey in the first place. From there he did go, finally, towards Oregon.

No doubt Fremont had heard that if the U.S. flag was raised in California, the citizens would thereupon rejoice and embrace it, or, if an Independent flag was raised, some similar felicity would take place. There had often been suggestions and hopes that one of these might happen. But if these were Fremont's notions, one ingredient was missing: tender diplomacy.

"Fremont's conduct in California during 1846 is one of the phenomena that mortals are unable to explain, for there is much in it of both good and bad."

—M.G. Vallejo

"After Fremont left Gavilan, Sr. Gillespie arrived at Monterey...Consul Larkin introduced him into Monterey society at a ball...we found it difficult to believe that the government of the United States would send a ship of war solely to bring a young invalid to California...We called

A grand Ball
April 19, 1846

this to Castro's attention, suggesting the idea that Gillespie was an emissary who came for no good and that it would be well to arrest him and send him to Mexico, but Castro told us that we were thinking ill of an invalid gentleman, accusing all the women in general of thinking ill of others, much more than the men. We answered that almost always we more often hit the mark."

—*Señora Jimeno Casarín Ord*

Arch. Gillespie, Gen. Castro
& Demon Rum

Lieutenant Archibald Gillespie, USMC

a gentleman in whom the president reposes entire confidence

The United States Sloop of War *Cyane* arrived at Monterey on April 18, 1846. In California a ball was given for almost every occasion. One was given the next day at Alvarado's house to honor Captain Dupont and his officers, who had made a very good impression upon the people of Monterey. Captain Dupont was surprised to hear about Fremont's activities.

The *Cyane* had brought a passenger, supposedly a civilian. Mr. Archibald Gillespie was introduced as a merchant from New York who had come to California for his health. In fact, he was a lieutenant of the U.S. Marines, sent on a secret mission by President Polk, with a message to Fremont, to be delivered no matter where he might be.

What was the dispatch to Fremont? Neither Gillespie or Fremont ever revealed it, but it was probably that war was going to break out with Mexico (it was declared on May 11th), that the United States intended to take California, and that Fremont was to take direction and make certain that our country and no other got California.

Overthrow the government, and conquer California at once!—was the message, according to Fremont's father-in-law, Senator Benton, who had been in on it with President Polk..

Alvarado's house was decorated for the ball, with the flags of Mexico and the United States "lovingly entwined." The music was the best in the capital, and the

Arch. Gillespie   Consul Larkin

supper was as good as could be. Gillespie knew Spanish very well, but he spoke little, and that badly. General Castro did not let him out of his sight, and every minute invited him to drink, to find out his secrets. Gillespie refused. Instead of dancing, he only chatted with Larkin. This made the Californians suspect the motives of the New York merchant who came to seek the pure air of California. The suspicions were turned into reality at two o'clock in the morning, when it was found that Gillespie had left the ball and was not to be found in Monterey. At six in the morning, Manuel Cantua, a messenger from Salvador Vallejo in Sonoma, arrived in Monterey and announced that he had met an American gentleman about twelve miles out from Monterey, accompanied by two vaqueros who worked for Larkin.

Gillespie arrived at San Francisco, and with the help of the American Vice Consul Leidesdorff, he rented a whale boat and in a short time arrived at New Helvetia. Here he met Captain Sutter, who was now an agent of Larkin's and in his debt for large amounts of goods bought on credit. Of course Captain Sutter gave a warm welcome to such a guest. He provided Gillespie with good guides, pack animals and horses, and his best $300 mule, and told him that Fremont should not be very far from the settlements of the fierce Klamath Indians.

Gillespie, considering the important correspondence he carried, hastened up and over the mountains after Fremont. "Hardships, narrow escapes, and want of food...with soft stones for beds," were endured. Gillespie's little party of six was attacked by the brave Klamaths, who were friendly to the British and unfriendly to the Americans. Sam Neal, who had been on Fremont's last expedition, went ahead with the best horse to find Fremont and help. With reins in his teeth, "he fired his rifle to port and starboard" as he charged through the bravest Indians they had ever seen.

Fremont and his men returned from Oregon with Gillespie, and camped near where Marysville is now. "Captain Fremont invites every freeman in the valley to come to his camp at the Buttes, immediately," he wrote on June 8 to every American there. The Americans hastened to Fremont's call, from whom they learned "the plan of conquest" of Alta California.

If we had not gone to meet Gillespie, he and party would have been murdered. Kit Carson

Sam Neal

Sigler

A fight with the Klamaths

"They are the bravest Indians we have ever seen." —*Fremont*

Fremont's
Camp on Bear Creek
June 10, 1846

Wm. B. Ide and J. C. Fremont

The Plan of Conquest

Select a dozen men who have nothing to lose, but everything to gain, encourage them to steal General Castro's horses and capture some of the principal Californians and make Castro strike the first blow in a war with the U.S. Then march home.

Captain Fremont explained the plan to Wm. B. Ide, and asked his opinion. Ide said, "Although beyond the protecting shield of the United States' flag, they still cherished the memory of the American name, the honor of which was yet dearer to them by far than any rewards of falsehood and treachery dishonorably won." Fremont answered as you see opposite.

Ide then talked with some of the men: "When the breach is once made, that involves us all...We are too few for division...Down on Sonoma! Never flee the country, nor give it up while there is an arm to fight, or a voice to cry aloud for Independence. But let truth and honor guide our course."

"Good," cried the men, "Hurrah for Independence."

But what was Castro doing? "*Señor* Castro I believe has gone North to raise a party against Pico," wrote Larkin on June first. Two weeks later Fremont was certain that Castro was after him: "I am in hourly expectation of the approach of General Castro," he wrote on June 16 from New Helvetia to Captain Montgomery. What happened in the meantime?

The Breech is Made
Fremont's Advice is Followed by Merritt
& a Little Band of Followers

"They will be subject, if they do not return voluntarily from the country, to be expelled from it whenever the government may find it convenient."

—M. Castro to Guerrero, April 30, 1846

A Californian, Lieutenant Francisco Arce, boasted at New Helvetia, it was said, that General Castro was going to expel all the Americans from the country. Once before American backwoodsmen had been arrested and sent in chains to Mexico; but Castro was put in jail there for this, and he would have been wiser now. Besides, Castro was going to fight Pio Pico, not the Americans. He had just told *Señor* Leese that he favored seeing the American flag fly in California, anyway.

But "scarcely a year passed when the story did not go forth that the Americans were to be expelled," and the Americans knew, like Machiavelli, that a good excuse can be made up for any naughty adventure. Arce was on his way to collect the Sonoma horses for Castro to mount his men, and these war preparations worried the Americans. They didn't think that they were intended for Pico, for Fremont's behavior had given Castro plenty of reason for going after him.

When the Californians fought Governor Micheltorena, the first thing they did was to drive away all his horses. Now near the Cosumnes River, twelve Americans led by Captain Merritt took Arce's 160 horses, just as the twelve Californians in charge were having their breakfast. Merritt, an old Rocky Mountain hunter, said that if Castro wanted the horses he could come and get them. Castro was at his headquarters in Santa Clara.

Early dawn on June 10, 1846

Semple, Ford & Merritt

Lt. Alviso

Lt. d'Arce

A Mission of Benevolence & Good Will
Towards the Sleeping & Unsuspecting Inhabitants of Sonoma

General Vallejo kept a guard posted at the door to see that everyone in passing his house took off his hat. The guard, suddenly, was captured. "About half past five in the morning of Sunday June 14th, 1846, a group of rough looking desperados had surrounded the house of General Vallejo and had arrested him, Captain Salvador Vallejo and Victor Prudhon (the General's brilliant secretary). General Vallejo, dressed in the uniform of a General of the Mexican Army, was the prisoner of this large group of rough-looking men, some wearing on their heads caps made with the skins of coyotes or wolves, some wearing slouched hats full of holes, some wearing straw hats as black as charcoal. The majority of this marauding band wore buckskin pants, some blue pants that reached only to the knee, several had no shirts; shoes were to be seen on the feet of fifteen or twenty among the whole lot."

—Señora Leese

Ezekiel Merritt   John Grigsby

Daybreak of the 14th
of June, 1846

Dr. Semple, Merritt, Mr. Knight -to all appearance the least inhuman of that god-forsaken crowd. Doña Rosalía

"After the first surprise had a little subsided, as no immediate violence was offered, the general's generous spirits gave proof of his usual hospitality—as the richest wines and brandies sparkled in the glasses...and those who had thus unceremonially met soon became merry companions, more especially, the merry visitors."

"While matters were going on thus happily in the house, the main force sat patiently guarding it without...The sun was climbing up the heavens an hour or more, and yet no man, or voice, nor sound of violence came from the house to tell us of the events within."

"Oh, go into the house, Ide, and come out again and let us know what is going on in there." No sooner said than done.

—*Ide*

General Vallejo was a lifelong teetotaler, and so was Mr. Ide, but. . .
"After the first surprise had a little subsided, as no immediate violence was offered,
The general's generous spirits gave proof of his usual hospitality."

"Thus and so was the 'INDEPENDENT BEAR FLAG REPUBLIC' inaugurated."
Thereafter "whiskey was altogether a contraband article."

Sonoma, 1840's   Salvador Vallejo's house   Gen. Vallejo's h

General and Captain Vallejo, Lt. Colonel Prudhon—and *Señor* Leese—were ordered to get ready to go to Captain Fremont's camp. Captain Ide told *Señor* Leese that Fremont had ordered the gentlemen brought to him. One hundred horses were also taken from Sonoma, including the Leese childrens'.

Don Pepe de la Rosa rode to Sausalito to describe the situation to Captain Montgomery on board the *Portsmouth. Don* Pepe asked that a U.S. officer come to Sonoma to save the helpless inhabitants from violence and anarchy. Captain Montgomery sent Lieutenant Misroon to tell the invaders to be kind to the good citizens of Sonoma. He also sent along his son, John Elliott Montgomery, Captain's clerk.

"You will say to General Vallejo on my part, that I at once and entirely disavow this movement as having proceeded under any authority of the U. States or myself, as the agent of my Government in this Country, or on this coast...I also disavow the same on the part of Capt. Fremont..."
—*Montgomery*

They were then delivered to the tender mercy of John A. Sutter, "the arch fiend," said *Señora* Leese.

Aboard the *Portsmouth* off
Rancho Sausalito
June 15, 1846

Clerk John E. Montgomery   Commander Montgomery   Don José de la Rosa   Lt. W. A. Bartlett, Interpreter

Barracks   San Francisco Solano

Because of the "immense influence of General Vallejo with his countrymen... this was a mere act of precaution," said Henry L. Ford. It was also "a gross and inexcusable outrage...a most ungenerous return for his many acts of kindness to American settlers, his influence in behalf of annexation to the United States."

(Bancroft)

"The Mexican flag was still flying at the top of the flagstaff...in the hustle of the morning it had been forgotten. It was now hauled down and it became necessary to put one of our own in its place. The lone star was thought of that belonged to Texas; they were determined to have a star, and tried to think of some other device to go with it. A piece of common domestic (cloth) was obtained and a man by the name of Todd proceeded to paint from a pot of red paint a star upon the corner of it. Before he had finished one of the party (said to have been Merritt, an old bear fighter) proposed to put on the center facing the star a grizzly bear. It was adopted unanimously..."

Sutter's Fort
Tuesday, June 16th, 1846
(his establishment grew
since you saw it last)

Leese

Gen. Vallejo

Grigsby

Sutter

Bidwell

"Arrived in the evening as prisoners General Vallejo, Salvador Vallejo, Prudon & Leese." *New Helvetia Diary*

It was his own design, and done for mere pastime. Bidwell

Mr. Todd paints the Flag

"It was taken to the flagstaff and hoisted amid the hurrahs of the little party who swore to defend it if need be with their lives."

—*Henry L. Ford*

"This day we proclaim California a Republic," said Ide the next day.

Of course this was not very popular with the Californians. *Señora* Vallejo had strong words to say about this scene: "They have hoisted to the flagpole a rag that has a bear painted on it and that is the same as saying that they are thieves. If you want peace to reign on the frontier, order that rag taken down and run up the American flag. Under the protection of that flag we may live peacefully and, perhaps, even united, for many of my sisters are married to Americans and you know that family

I have some doubt if anyone can tell the exact day it was raised. Bidwell

It was on the 14th of June, '46

CALIFORNIA REPUBLIC.

We are few, but we are firm and true. Ide

"We were no base band of robbers, bent on mischief."
Ide

*The Bears intend
no violence.*

The utmost harmony & good order prevail in the Camp.
Lt. John S. Missroon, June 17, 1846

ties are very strong." Pio Pico said stronger things: "A gang of North American Adventurers, with the blackest treason which the spirit of the devil could invent, have invaded the post of Sonoma displaying their flag and making prisoners of four Mexican citizens...The North American Nation,...putting in execution her piratical intentions, has robbed us of the Department of Texas and wishes to do the same with California." He was "satisfied that Great Britain would give California protection."

The next day, June 15, a junta of Californian officers was to meet in Santa Barbara, "to devise some means to reinstate the deplorable affairs of this Country." Fremont said that he would be there, too, (of course he hadn't been invited) and Montgomery offered to send along the *Portsmouth*. The British Vice Consul was there, and HMS *Juno* was on the way. Who would win California?

Fremont comes to Sonoma

"In the 25th of June, at 2 P.M., came Captain Fremont with the whole of his forces, amounting to 72 men. He said that he had come down, not to take any part in the matter, but only to see the sport, and explore about the Bay." —*Ide*. On the 26th this "pleasure party" left—about 134 men now, for San Rafael, where the Californian army was expected. Fremont now led "Americans, French, English, Swiss, Poles, Russians, Prussians, Chilians, Germans, Greeks, Austrians, Pawnees, native Indians, etc.," said James Marshall.

Capt. Ide

Capt. Fremont

Kit Carson

After the fort (Sonoma) had been taken, Fremont had heard positively of the war being declared. He then marched forward to Sonoma, and found it in the possession of the men he had sent in advance. —Kit Carson

Captain Ide, the Bearflag chief, had set up his headquarters at the Leese house. *Señoras* Vallejo and Leese had sent a cart full of firearms to Juan Padilla, Ramon Carrillo and his honored mother, who were organizing the rancheros to come and rescue Sonoma. Captain Ide had come into the room where the *señoras* were conversing and told them that unless they sent letters to Padilla and Carrillo, begging them not to approach Sonoma, he would shut them up in a room and kill them as soon as the Californians came in sight over the Sonoma hills. "Four ill-looking desperados stood near me with drawn pistols." said *Señora* Leese. "I wrote the fatal letter," as Rosie helped compose it.

Señora Vallejo asked Ide for a passport for the messenger, Gervasio, to take the letter to the Californians. Gervasio travelled with his oxcart filled with hides, and among the hides the *señoras* placed a dozen pistols, ten pounds of powder, four flintlocks and six sabers. With these and the letter, Gervasio left in the direction of Petaluma. On the way he met Padilla and Carrillo and gave them the arms.

The Clever Ruse
(and a Wild Goose Chase)

Captain Fremont and his men had gone to San Rafael to look for the Californians. Fremont's "charge upon the deserted old Mission of San Rafael, every man

Rosie Leese, *Señoras* Leese and Vallejo —and four ill-looking desperados

yelling, whooping, swinging his hat, as the whole body put their horses to the fullest speed and coming right up to the front of the venerable old structure, was spoken of at the time as something curious, if not thrilling," wrote Bidwell, one of the men.

A letter was intercepted on the evening of the 28th of June, saying that early on the morning of the 30th the Californians would invade Sonoma. The Bears were as nervous as could be. About 4:00 A.M. the tramping of horses was heard, and they were sure the Californians were upon them. "The blankets of the advancing host flowed in the breeze...the impatience of the men at the guns became intense. 'My God! they swing the matches!' cried the well known voice of Kit Carson. 'Hold on, hold on! 'tis Fremont, 'tis Fremont!' " Then it was they saw the ruse. A clever letter had made Fremont return to Sonoma and let the Californians escape him; it had almost made the Bearflagmen fire on Fremont. Fremont didn't write about this because "his writing utensils were left at San Rafael," said Gillespie.

Now Fremont really wanted Carrillo's head, and he sent people looking all through the woods for him. Carrillo wrote to his sister from Mount Petaluma on June 22; he had assembled the neighbors and the armed Indians only to claim the peace promised by Ide's proclamation, he said. The Sonoma ladies thought he'd be safest with them, right under the noses of Fremont and the Bears. *Don* Ramon came into the town unseen in Gervasio's oxcart, past the guards, and was hidden in the attic of Vallejo's big house until the flag of the United States was raised in the Plaza.

Fremont's Charge on San Rafael
June 26, 1846

Sonoma, 4:00 A.M. June 30, 1846

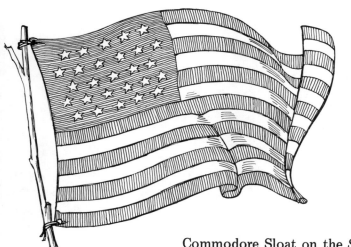

The Stars & Stripes

Commodore Sloat on the *Savannah* arrived at Monterey on July 2nd. He knew that there was war with Mexico, but Consul Larkin told him the Californians might raise the U.S. flag themselves, so the commodore waited. But finally he told Larkin, "We must take the place! I shall be blamed for doing too little or too much—I prefer the latter." He also knew that Admiral Seymour was on his way with HMS *Collingwood*, and might raise the British flag, and that Fremont was fighting the Californians *with orders from Washington*, according to a letter from Timothy Murphy. So at 10:00 A.M., July 7, 1846, the American flag was raised at the Monterey customshouse "amid the hurrahs of the people, who were pleased to see waving in the old capital a flag which Thomas O. Larkin has taught them to regard as a symbol of the most unalloyed liberty," wrote General Vallejo. "I come as the best friend of California," Sloat wrote Pico; "a great increase in the value of real estate... may also be anticipated," said his Proclamation.

July 9th: the United States flag was ordered raised at Yerba Buena by Commander Montgomery of the *Portsmouth;* Paul Revere's grandson, Lieutenant Joseph Warren Revere, was sent to Sonoma "to put the American flag on the staff where before was the Bear...He carried out his mission amid the thunderous cheers of all the Californians who resided at Sonoma," said Vallejo, who was still in Sutter's jail. A little later, the soiled Bear Flag was presented by one of the Bears to Montgomery's sixteen year old son, the captain's clerk, John Elliott Montgomery. He described it in a letter to his mother:

"Their Flag consisted of a Star Union with a Grizzly bear in the center looking up at the star and under the Bear the words "Republic of California"; on the lower border there was a red Stripe of Flannel. The whole was composed of a piece of white cotton & Black berry juice (& Brick dust and oil) there being no paint in the country. I have the original & only Flag of the Californian Republic in my possession & esteem it quite a prize."   *John Elliott Montgomery*, July 25, 1846

Lieutenant Revere caused some misunderstanding about the Bear Flag because he later described it with "a Bear rampant" (prancing on its hind legs), which it was not. From Sonoma Lieutenant Revere sent an American flag to be raised at Sutter's Fort on July 10th, to replace the "Lone Star" flag that had recently been flying there, made from the flag of the former regime; it probably had a Bear painted on it, too.

"Having received a flag from Commodore Sloat, we proceeded to raise it over the Pueblo at the *Juzgado* near *El Dorado* Street," wrote Fallon from San Jose on July 14th. But the flag pole had been stolen, so a very, very crooked one was quickly fashioned for the occasion.

"Cuffy (the Bear) came down growling."
John Elliott Montgomery

"Great satisfaction appeared to prevail in the community of Sonoma."
Lt. *Joseph W. Revere*

Rosie Leese

Lt. Revere

CALIFORNIA

Capt. Grigsby

"The flag of the U States was displayed at Sonoma at meridian on the same day July 9." *Jn. B. Montgomery*

Pio Pico sent word to the Supreme Government in Mexico City that if Mexico wouldn't send proper protection, California would rebel and seek the protection of Her Britannic Majesty. Santa Anna wouldn't send aid to "those distant States" (other northern states of Mexico were rebelling, too) as his own army needed all its resources. Pico was a Californian, which was to say not a truly loyal son of Mexico. "The few Mexicans in the Department," wrote José Maria Flores, Castro's soon-to-be successor, "had to tolerate shameful actions by the Californians, who manifested an all-consuming hatred against them. "The governor, as well as Castro, are agreed on one thing, that no one from Mexico shall ever be governor" in California, he added. So there was little love lost in Mexico for the ever-revolting Californians. Pico sent a request for help to the British fleet at Mazatlán, and Admiral Seymour was agreeable.

But it was nine days after the U.S. flag was raised at Monterey that the British flagship *Collingwood* came belatedly into Monterey Bay. From the officers of that ship, it was learned, "that as they rounded the point and the United States men-of-war were discovered and the American flag came in sight, floating over the town, the British admiral stamped his foot in rage and flung his hat upon the deck. His chagrin at the advantage which the Americans had gained over him in this matter caused these demonstrations." The Britons in California had all been certain until then that the country would shortly become part of the British Empire. M. Gasquet, the French consul, had also been momentarily expecting a French squadron at Monterey. He protested against American activity to Sloat; but he protested too much. Sloat sent three cabin boys to arrest him.

In truth, Monterey (and Los Angeles later) was conquered by music; "over 100 marines with their music paraded the town today, to which will be added next 16 more musicians and soon after 18 more making 40 in the 'Band,' " wrote Larkin on July 8. "These Californians are extravagantly fond of music. A full band was never heard before in the country (except Jones'), and it was amusing to see its effect in drawing them out of their hiding-places," said Captain Phelps.

"The Tenure under which the Forces of the United States at present hold this province should be regarded as provisional."
G. F. Seymour, Rear Admiral & Commander in Chief of Her Britannic Majesty's Pacific Squadron

The Sonoma prisoners were released from Sutter's fortress, and the "uncouth Missourian" who guarded them repented. General Vallejo had for years wanted the change which had just taken place. Mr. Leese, back in the bosom of his family with Rosie at his side, looked after his vineyard near Sonoma; the grapes were "as lucious, I dare say, as the forbidden fruit that provoked the first transgression. Nothing can exceed the delicious richness and flavor of the California grape," wrote *Alcalde* Bryant when he visited there. Gen. Vallejo had planted some 400 vines in 1834, behind his *Casa Grande* (the Cheese Factory is now there). Soon he would plant hundreds more, and turn the old barracks into a splendid wine cellar. He would win a beautiful medal at San Francisco's first agricultural fair, and many awards afterwards.

Rosie Leese by Mt. Tamalpais,
going to the fiesta

" Oh, what a proud day for Yerba Buena!"

Commodore Stockton replaced Commodore Sloat as commander of the Pacific Squadron, and as governor, and on October 5 there was to be a Grand Reception for him in Yerba Buena—and, of course, a Grand Reception Ball. There had been continuous balls at Mr. Leidesdorff's house since the Stars and Stripes were raised, but there was never anything like the one for his Excellency the new Yankee governor. The excellent Marine Band from the ships *Savannah* and *Portsmouth*, dressed in glorious red jackets, played all day parading up one street and down the other one, and now they would play all night and until morning at the Grand Reception Ball. All the dignitaries were there: Captain Paty colorfully dressed in his splendid uniform of the Hawaiian Navy, a Russian Commander, a French Commander, General Vallejo and the rancheros from all around the Bay, *Alcalde* Bartlette, Captain Montgomery (who had just arrived), officers, sailors were there, and all the Californian ladies were presented to his Excellency.

"Talk of your Dignity Balls, your Ball *en masque*, your Fancy Balls, and your Fourth of July Balls—pshaw. There never was a Ball given since Noah first landed from the ark that could compare in all its details with the ' Reception Ball ' at Yerba Buena. The Large Dining Room of the largest house in the city was most

The Grand Reception Ball

If father buys land out here, I shall want to stay here; it is a lovely climate & country.
—J. E. Montgomery

Blue naval uniforms with gilt epaulettes and buttons; bright red coatees on the Marine bandsmen, with yellow tape on collars & cuffs; yellow epaulettes; brass belt buckles, white trousers and belts; black shako (cap) with yellow plume and brass badge and strap.

brilliantly illuminated, and shone forth in all the blaze and brilliancy of 100 candles, which reflected from some 30 or 40 mirrors..." Sailor Downey of the *Portsmouth* described it all. And here Rosalía Leese dances with young John Elliott Montgomery.

TRUE ROMANCE should have accelerated here; but, alas, young Montgomery was lost—either murdered or lost in a storm—about November 13, 1846. His brother was master of the *Warren*, and the launch from that ship was sent up the Sacramento River to Sutter's Fort with a big payroll. John Elliott went along to see the sights, and he and his brother and the ten sailors, along with the money, were never seen again. He had just written his mother that he was "going to buy 2 square leagues of land here," to try his luck at farming. Rosie died five years later.

Flags of the War

Flag of Fremont's California Battalion
of Mounted Riflemen

The Americans had just taken a beating at Gomez' rancho, by the Salinas River. Captain Burroughs was dead, and his men were hemmed in. On the morning of November 18, 1846, a column of mounted horsemen appeared in the distance, and the Americans thought it was the enemy coming back. "A flag was borne at the head of the advancing troop, and we vainly endeavored to cheat ourselves that it was the red, white, and blue, and that these were our friends coming to our relief. We made ourselves ready for battle...Nearer they came, and thicker arose the doubts and questionings of their true character. But while we were watching and waiting with beating hearts, the distant notes of a bugle fell on our ears. Now we could hear them rise and fall in lively cadence, and now every mother's son of that motley group threw up his hand or his hat in joyful recognition of the old tune, for the strains we heard were *Yankee Doodle*. Our suspense was ended, and the relief for which we had so anxiously waited had come. The strange flag borne by the advancing battalion was not our country's colors, but an eagle painted on a square field of blue."

Trooper: navy blue shirt with white stars & trim on the collar: buckskin trousers, red hatband; flag: blue field, red, white & blue U.S. flags & shield; brown eagle.

Flag of the Mormon Battalion

"We are true-hearted Americans . . . ready to enter the field of battle." *Elder Little*, 1846

Colors: white field, red stripes alternating with white; red top of M, bottom of O, top of R, bottom of M, top of O, bottom of N, shading of L and O in Lion, face of 1 in 1847; shaded front parts of letters and numbers are blue; all other parts such as sides of letters and numbers, are yellow; yellow stars.

It was said that the U.S. government made an offer in 1843 to Joseph Smith, to raise a Mormon army to conquer California. Early in 1846 two Mormon groups left the U.S. for California, one by land and the other, led by Elder Brannan, around Cape Horn on the *Brooklyn*. The Mormons hadn't yet decided where in the west they'd settle, but California was where Brigham Young had "fixed his attention." The *Brooklyn* arrived at Yerba Buena on August 2nd 1846 to find the U.S. flag flying. The Mormons had come well armed, and had drilled while at sea, and they were expecting to take the place themselves. "They had a flag of their own, but as it was not unfurled in California I cannot describe it." wrote Capt. Phelps. We wish that he could have, but when Brigham Young was asked later what his flag looked like, he replied that it was the flag of the United States.

While the *Brooklyn* had been at sea, 500 Mormon Volunteers were recruited by Brigham Young himself, to form the Mormon Battalion to serve in California. The troops, assembled in two weeks, left Council Bluffs on July 20, 1846. They made an incredible march of 1,100 miles down the burning Santa Fe Trail; there were bad water, wild bulls, terrible mountains, constant exhaustion. They reached San Diego on January 29, 1847, "half-naked, half-fed." The war was just over. Guard duty began; in San Diego, "the Mormons.... effected a kind of industrial revolution." Many who had been in the Battalion became important later in California's history, and several discharged Mormons were with James Marshall when gold was discovered.

This intriguing flag is located at the Pioneer Museum in Farmington, Utah. The word *Battalion* is misspelled, it is thought, to punctuate the word *lion*, which is what Brigham Young was called.

YERBA BUENA COMPANY
SEMPER PARATUS
OF VOLUNTEERS

This flag is a reconstruction,
and the colors are not known.

The stars and the stripes are said to represent the companies of the battalion. The flag was presented by the grandson of the boy who mixed the dyes, painted the flag on a sheet, and carried it across the mountains. We would like to learn more about it.

Flag of the
Yerba Buena Volunteers
& Lt. Washington A. Bartlett, USN
Alcalde of Yerba Buena
January 12, 1847

"Lt. Bartlett of the Navy had been appointed *Alcalde* of Yerba Buena and held his courts, & decided the most intricate & difficult questions of Spanish law. He gave much offense by some of his legal decisions. A man was arrested & thrown into prison because his name was Sanchez, and a person named Sanchez had rendered himself very conspicuous in his hostility to the Americans, so the unfortunate was imprisoned because he bore the same name, & must be a relative of the other."

The *Alcalde* one day fell into the hands of the Sanchez family and they measured out to him the same justice which he had been meting to them and their countrymen. He is closely detained as a prisoner."

—*Lt. Craven, USS* Dale, *1847*

So Captain Ward Marston of the marines led an expedition down the peninsula against Sanchez. Captain Smith led the Yerba Buena Volunteers to free their *Alcalde*. There was a little battle at Santa Clara; a conference followed: Bartlett was given up and the Americans agreed to behave better, more or less.

Flag of the N.Y. Volunteers

President Polk "determined to send a regiment of volunteers around Cape Horn to the Pacific," to help conquer California. Congress had authorized him to do this on May 13, 1846. Colonel Johnathan Stevenson of New York City was asked to organize such a regiment of "persons of good habits," who'd want to remain in California after the war. "The mask is off; the veil is lifted; and we see in the clearest characters invasion, conquest, and colonization emblazoned on our banners," said a Massachusetts congressman. But the banner of the 1st Regiment of N.Y. Volunteers was the N.Y. State flag, presented by a "news collector" for the *New York Herald* as the ships departed—just as a sheriff's posse was coming to arrest the colonel. It had been sent by a now "checkmated villain" who had wanted the command, and who had used a silly law suit to try to get it. The regiment arrived in California in March 1847.

"The uniform of the regiment...is very neat and serviceable; pantaloons of dark mixed gray with a scarlet stripe or cord up the seam of the leg, blue coats with scarlet trimmings, a new style of French cap, very becoming."   *N.Y. Herald,* 1846

Blue field of flag, sky on shield, coat & cap; white ribbon with motto & sword belt; brown eagle & mountains; yellow sun, other scrolls, fallen crown, epaulettes, cap trim, belt badge; red cuffs, sash, collar fronts.